Adventures with *Barbie*™ 3

Wildlife Rescue

Stephanie St. Pierre

PRICE STERN SLOAN
Los Angeles

For Mom and Dad

with love

Published by Price Stern Sloan, Inc.
11150 Olympic Boulevard
Los Angeles, California 90064
ISBN: 0-8431-2918-2
Printed in the United States of America
10 9 8 7 6 5 4 3 2

Contents

Africa!

"Oh, look!" Barbie said. She and Kira and Ken were on an airplane. They were about to land in Africa. "This is so exciting!" said Barbie. "I can't wait to get there and see everything."

"Our guide should be meeting us when we get off the plane," said Kira. She had asked Barbie and Ken to come with her to Africa. They wanted to try to help save the wild animals there.

Animals like lions, elephants and rhinos were in danger. Sometimes the animals were hunted. Sometimes they just didn't have room to live as cities grew bigger and bigger. Many people wanted to help the animals. They made huge parks, called game reserves, where the animals could live safely.

"Will we be taking photographs today?" Ken asked. Kira was going to take lots of pictures of the wild animals. The pictures would be used for a calendar that would be sold to raise money to protect the animals. They had only a week for their trip so they would be very busy.

"I think we'll be too busy finding a campsite and setting up our tents," Kira said. "Today will be just for fun."

"Tomorrow we'll get to work then," said Barbie. She would be modeling in some of the photographs. She might even take some pictures herself.

"And tonight, we'll be camping out under the African sky," said Kira.

"I can't wait to see the stars!" Barbie said.

Finally their plane landed. As soon as they got off the plane they saw their guide. He was holding a sign that said BARBIE AND COMPANY on it. They waved and he came to greet them.

"Hello," he said. "My name is Jim. Come this

way to get your bags." Before long they were loading their things into the back of a car called a Land Rover. The car was already packed with two big tents and lots of supplies.

"First the Director of Wildlife Services wants to meet you," said Jim as they drove into the city. "We will stop there on the way to the reserve. And you can change your clothes there too." It was very hot in Africa, too hot to wear the clothes they'd put on back home.

"Welcome to Africa," the Director said when they arrived in his office. "There's one important thing I need to discuss with you. We have had a lot of poachers going after elephants in the reserve. Be very careful."

"Are the poachers dangerous?" asked Ken.

"Yes," said the Director. "Especially to the elephants."

"Why are the poachers after the elephants?" Barbie asked.

"For their ivory tusks," said the Director.

"The ivory is carved to make jewelry and statues and other objects."

"And the elephants die for that?" asked Kira. It didn't seem fair.

"It's very sad," said the Director. "We hope the work you do will make the reserve safer for elephants. And for all the other wild animals we are trying to save."

"Then we'd better get going," said Barbie. The Director showed them to rooms where they could change their clothes. Soon they were dressed in shorts, T-shirts, hats and hiking boots.

"Have a safe trip!" said the Director.

It was a long, hot drive. But the three friends enjoyed seeing the exciting new country, and Jim was a good guide. Once they reached the reserve, the road grew bumpy.

"Where are all the animals?" wondered Barbie. She looked out at the fields of tall grass. A tree stuck up here and there.

Sometimes they passed a thick clump of bushes and taller trees.

"Look!" Ken said. He pointed out his window. "A pride of lions."

"How beautiful," said Barbie. Jim stopped the Land Rover. Everyone stood up to look through the open-roof hatches. Three lions lay in the grass nearby. Four cubs tumbled around the grown lions.

"This calls for a picture," said Kira. She reached inside the car to get her camera. As she did, she noticed a large van speeding down the road toward them.

"Hey, look out!" she called. For a moment it seemed as if the van would run into them. It didn't slow down a bit.

"What's going on?" shouted Barbie. She and Ken and Jim ducked back inside the Land Rover. The driver of the van honked his horn and yelled at Barbie and her friends. He turned just in time to keep from hitting them.

"I think we've had our first meeting with poachers," said Jim. Everyone stared after the disappearing van.

2

Setting Up Camp

"Maybe we should follow him," said Barbie. "He scared away the lions." She sadly looked out at the empty field. "There's no reason to stay here."

"It's too dangerous," said Kira.

"Besides, he's too far away now," said Ken. "We'd never catch him."

"Let's just hope we don't run into him later," said Jim. "He's probably on his way to meet a poaching group."

They drove on. When the group reached their campsite, they were all hungry and thirsty and tired. It was late in the afternoon. But they wanted to set up their tents before lunch.

"I didn't know this was going to be such hard work," said Barbie when everything was unpacked and set up. "I'm starved."

"Me, too," said Kira.

Barbie and Kira left their tent and found Ken and Jim outside unpacking sandwiches from a large cooler. They had set up a table and chairs under a shady tree.

"Food!" cried the girls.

"Tonight we will cook over a campfire," said Jim. "But I thought something quicker might be good now."

"Sandwiches are perfect," said Barbie. She got one and sat down. "Will we be able to go out for a hike after we eat?" Barbie asked.

"Maybe a short one," said Jim. "We want to be in camp when it gets dark though."

"Are there dangerous animals out after dark?" asked Kira.

"Some," said Jim. "But there are also the poachers to worry about. And it is easy to get lost in the dark."

"I wonder what ever happened to that man in the van," said Barbie.

"By now he's met up with the rest of his group," said Jim.

"It makes me angry to think they could be hurting animals," said Barbie.

"And there's nothing we can do about it," said Ken.

"We could call the reserve rangers," Barbie said. "We've got the radio."

"What can we tell them?" Jim said. "I think we should not call unless we know something for sure."

"Like where the poachers are, or what they are poaching?" said Ken.

"Yes," said Jim.

"I guess that makes sense," said Barbie. She looked out across the tall grass. Here and there the funny bent trees stood up from the grass. But there wasn't an animal in sight.

"I hope we'll have better luck finding some animals tomorrow," said Kira. "I need to start taking pictures."

"We will find plenty of animals," said Jim. "Lions, giraffes, elephants, gazelles, even rhinos if we are lucky. But we need to hike farther into the bush."

"Are the animals afraid of people?" asked Ken.

"Some are more afraid than others," said Jim. "And they learn to stay away from places where the hunters go often."

"Look!" shouted Barbie. She jumped from her chair and pointed out toward the horizon. "The poachers' van." It was the same van that had almost run them off the road before. Now it was speeding through the grass.

"What are they doing?" said Kira.

"It looks as if they're trying to get away from someone," said Ken. The van sped into a bunch of trees and disappeared.

"They must be trying to get out of the reserve," said Jim. "If they make it through those trees, they'll come out near the main entrance."

"Now we have to use that radio," said Barbie. "We can warn the rangers." She hurried into the tent and turned the radio on.

"Thanks for the help," said the ranger at the other end. "Maybe we'll catch them now."

"I'm glad we could help," said Barbie. "Let us know what happens." The ranger signed off.

"Good work, Barbie," said Ken. Everyone went back outside to finish eating.

"Oh dear," said Kira.

"It looks like we've had visitors," said Jim. All the food was gone. Plastic wrappers and paper napkins were on the ground. Two chairs were knocked over. Soda cans had spilled all over the table and on the ground. It was a mess.

"Our lunch," said Barbie sadly. "But who could have taken it?" There wasn't anyone around for miles. Or was there?

3

One Big Baby

"Listen," said Jim. Everyone was quiet. At first they didn't hear a thing. Then they heard the sound of someone, or something, moving in the bushes.

"What is it?" said Barbie.

"Probably a hyena," said Jim. "They don't usually come so close to camp. But it's been a bad year. There is not enough food for them."

"So he smelled our lunch, and when we weren't looking he grabbed it," said Ken.

"I think so," said Jim. "Of course, it could be a larger animal. If we go back into the tents, we might see what it is."

"This could be a great chance to take some pictures," Kira said. She and Barbie went to their tent and got their cameras ready. They knelt near their open tent flap and watched the bushes.

"Look," Barbie whispered. "Something's moving those leaves!" As they watched, slowly a large gray shape appeared.

"A baby elephant!" said Kira. She quickly started snapping photos. So did Barbie.

"Can we go near it?" Barbie wondered. She wished Jim wasn't in the other tent with Ken. He would know if it was safe to go near the animal. For now Barbie would have to wait and take some more pictures. The elephant walked back to the table. It picked up a soda can with its trunk and held it to its mouth. When it tasted the soda it snorted and threw down the can. The girls couldn't help laughing.

"He doesn't like diet soda," said Barbie with a giggle.

"Oh, look," said Kira. Jim had come out of his tent and was slowly moving toward the elephant. It stopped when it saw him, but didn't run away. Jim was a few feet from the

creature when the baby elephant lifted his trunk and trumpeted. He was warning Jim to stay away.

"Do you think Jim is in trouble?" Kira asked.

"I think the worst that elephant could do is step on him," said Barbie. "I think it's just scared." Jim held out a pail full of water. He spilled a little water in front of the animal and set the pail down.

"Look, he's drinking it," Barbie said. As the girls watched him, they saw there was a large cut on the baby elephant's back. It was bleeding a little.

"The poor thing," said Barbie. "What could have happened to him?"

"Maybe it got away from those awful poachers," said Kira.

"You're probably right," said Barbie. "I wonder where its mother is?" Jim moved closer and closer to the elephant until he was able to gently stroke its ear. At first the elephant looked worried, but soon it calmed down. Jim spoke quiet words as he petted him.

"This will make a super shot," said Kira. She kept snapping photos. "I'll bet Jim didn't expect to be a model." Barbie laughed. She really wanted to get closer to the baby elephant. Slowly she moved through the tent flap until she was standing outside the tent. Jim saw her and waved her over.

"Hi there, baby," she said quietly when she got close enough to touch the elephant. Now she could see that he looked very tired and dirty. His skin was scratched and muddy.

"I think he escaped from the poachers," said Jim. "I can't explain what happened to his family."

"That's horrible," said Barbie. It made her upset to think this baby elephant might be an orphan. "What can we do for him?"

"First we should give him plenty of water and show him we mean no harm," said Jim.

"Then we must clean the blood off him. If we don't, he won't last long."

"What do you mean?" Barbie asked. She stroked the elephant's forehead. He closed his eyes.

"Other animals will smell the blood and hunt him down," said Jim. "If we can wash him off and keep him in camp tonight, he might be all right by morning."

"Let's do it then," said Barbie. She smiled at the elephant. "Poor baby," she said. The elephant looked calm now. He seemed happy to have Jim and Barbie nearby.

"A baby elephant likes company," said Jim. "You stay with him while we get more water."

"No problem," said Barbie. She was happy to babysit this baby. Kira and Ken followed Jim to the Land Rover. He took out three jugs to fill with water.

"We'll be back in five minutes," he said. Then he and Barbie's friends left to get the water.

"I guess it's just me and you," Barbie said to the little elephant. He lifted his trunk and made a funny snorting sound. Barbie patted his forehead again and he closed his eyes. Barbie laughed when she realized the baby elephant had fallen asleep.

4

A Cry in the Dark

Barbie sat in the grass near the sleeping elephant. She wondered what had happened to this baby's mother. Maybe tomorrow they could find out.

"And what's going to happen to you?" Barbie wondered out loud. The baby elephant couldn't live on his own. A sound in the bushes startled Barbie. She jumped up and surprised the elephant, who started to trumpet. He was frightened.

"It's only us," said a familiar voice. Ken came through the bushes first. He was carrying a full water jug.

"Calm down," Barbie said to the elephant. She patted his head. Soon the elephant was quiet again.

"Poor elephant," said Kira. "You've had such

a bad time." She brought a large cooking pot out of the tent and filled it with water. When she put it down on the ground, the elephant drank it all up in a minute.

"How much water do you think he's going to drink?" Kira asked. She had found a large wash tub. "Should we fill this tub?"

"That will be just right," said Jim. "When he is finished drinking, he will spray himself with the water. We can help him to wash the dust off his skin. We can clean his wound too." The group watched as the elephant began to fill his trunk with water and then spray it back out over his head.

"He's feeling better," said Barbie.

"Once he is cleaned up," said Jim, "we should give him some leaves and tree bark to eat. That will be better for him than ham and cheese sandwiches." Everyone laughed.

"That reminds me," said Ken. "I'm still hungry."

"I didn't get much to eat before our visitor

arrived either," said Barbie.

"Well," said Jim. "Then we'd better get a fire built and start cooking supper. Maybe we will be able to eat by dinnertime."

Since there was so little firewood to be found in the reserve Jim set up the stove.

"If you would like to have a campfire, then you should look in the brush for some dead wood," Jim said.

"It would be nice to sit around a fire and sing songs tonight, wouldn't it?" Barbie said.

"Yes!" said Kira.

"A fire will also keep other animals away from the elephant," said Jim.

"I'll help gather wood," said Ken. He and Barbie left camp and walked through the thick clumps of bushes looking for pieces of wood.

"It's an amazing place, isn't it?" Barbie said. "So beautiful."

"Look at the sunset," Ken said. The sky

seemed huge. It was full of gold and pink and purple.

"And there's the wishing star," said Barbie. One bright star began to shine near the horizon. Barbie closed her eyes for a moment and made a wish.

"What did you wish for?" asked Ken.

"If I tell, it won't come true," said Barbie. She smiled at her friend and winked. "We'd better get going before it gets dark."

"I think we have enough wood now anyway," said Ken. The two friends watched the sky a few moments longer and then began walking back to their campsite. It was nearly dark when they arrived.

"Oh, you're back," said Kira. "I was beginning to worry."

"Sorry," said Barbie. "We stopped to watch the sunset."

"It is wonderful," Kira said.

"Mmm," said Barbie. "Something <u>smells</u>

wonderful around here." She walked over to the stove where Jim was stirring a big pot of stew.

"And you are just in time to eat it," said Jim. Plates and silverware appeared. Everyone took a big helping of the yummy stew and some flat African bread. They sat at the table eating.

"What about our baby elephant?" asked Barbie.

"He's munching on a nice fresh pile of leaves and branches," said Kira. "And he seems happy now that he's all cleaned up. We tied him to a tree so he can't wander off." Barbie was about to ask Kira what it had been like giving the elephant a bath when she heard a strange sound.

"What's that?" she cried.

"Who's there?" called Jim. Everyone jumped from the table as their questions were answered by a high-pitched scream.

5

Campfire Songs

It was the elephant. He was afraid of something. Barbie got to him first.

"What are you doing?" she called. A tall man in ragged clothes was trying to pull the baby elephant by the rope around his neck. But the elephant wouldn't move.

"None of your business," shouted the man. "Go away before you get hurt." He glared at Barbie. He looked very mean.

Suddenly there was a flash of bright light. Then another and another. The man dropped his rope and started running. Soon he disappeared into the dark. Jim laughed loudly.

"Shouldn't we go after him?" Barbie asked.

"We don't need to," said Kira. She held up her camera.

"You got pictures of him trying to steal the

elephant!" said Barbie.

"Yes, and we can give them to the rangers," said Kira. "Then the next time they see him, they'll keep a close watch on him."

"Hey, maybe we should just try to photograph the poachers on our trip and forget about the animals," joked Barbie.

"That is not a bad idea," said Jim with a smile. "But we should be careful now. The poachers will be very angry with us. We don't know if this man was one of the group we saw today, but he might be."

"I wonder what happened with that van," said Barbie. "Let's call the rangers' station and find out." They all hurried into the tent with the radio. When they got the ranger station, they asked about the poachers' van.

"We stopped the van," said the ranger. "But three of the men ran off into the bush. We caught only the driver. We took their load of ivory from them though."

"Thanks a lot," said Barbie. Everyone felt sad as they walked back to their dinner table. If the poachers had ivory, then it meant that elephants had died.

"Do you think our elephant has any family left?" Barbie asked Jim.

"Could we try to find them?" asked Kira.

"We can try," said Jim. "In the morning we can let him go and see where he takes us. He will probably try to find them on his own. Maybe we can help."

"But what if we don't find any other elephants?" asked Kira.

"He can't stay alone," said Jim. "He wouldn't last more than a few days."

"Is there a vet or a zoo or someplace we could take him?" Barbie asked. "Couldn't he stay somewhere until his back heals?"

"We can go into the city and talk to the Director," said Jim. "He will know what to do."

"But we can't leave the elephant here alone,"

said Barbie.

"You're right," said Jim. "Maybe you and Kira should go to the city."

"Jim and I can keep an eye on the elephant," said Ken.

"That's a good plan," said Barbie.

"And I can take care of that film too," said Kira.

"I'm sorry, Jim," said Barbie. "This stew was really good, but I'm too tired to eat now." No one was hungry.

"Why do we keep having interruptions at mealtimes?" said Ken.

"Maybe breakfast will be a quieter meal," Jim said.

"Let's light a campfire and sing a little before we go to bed," said Barbie.

"That's a great idea," said Kira. Soon they were sitting around the fire. They took turns teaching each other good songs. Jim sang a beautiful African song about the animals and the land.

"I love this song," said Barbie. Jim explained what the words meant. "Maybe I could do a record of it," she said. "It would be another way to tell people about what's happening to these poor animals."

"It would be very nice if you would sing the song," said Jim. "I can help you with the words if you want to sing it in my African language too." When it was time for bed, Barbie went to her tent humming the tune.

It was quiet in the tent. Then one long, sad call from the baby elephant filled the night.

"He must be very lonely tonight," said Barbie. "I hope we can find him a family soon."

"Me too," said Kira. The girls fell asleep dreaming of elephants and lions in the tall yellow grass.

6

Stop, Thief!

First thing in the morning, after a quiet breakfast, Barbie and Kira set off in the Land Rover.

"I hope we can get everything done quickly," said Barbie.

"Yes," said Kira. "It would be nice if we got back to the reserve in time to go out hiking." The drive into the city went fast. Along the way they saw zebras and Cape buffalo. They stopped to take pictures and still got to the city on time.

They had radioed a message to the Director. He was happy to see them when they arrived.

"I'm afraid we have some bad news," Barbie said. She and Kira told him the story of the poor baby elephant they had found. "We don't know what to do with the elephant if we can't find his herd," Barbie said.

"Hmm," said the Director. He thought for a while. "I'll make some phone calls to find out where he could be placed. But don't worry. I'm sure we'll find a place in the next few days."

"But what should we do until then?" Barbie asked.

"Can you keep the elephant?" asked the Director. "If he is happy, let him stay a few more days."

"It's okay with me," said Barbie.

"Me too," said Kira. "Except we won't be able to leave camp to take pictures."

"On the other hand, we can take lots and lots of baby elephant pictures!" said Barbie. The Director promised to radio them as soon as he found a place for the elephant. Barbie and Kira left to pick up the developed pictures.

"These are great," Kira said. The girls were standing near their Land Rover, looking at the pictures. They planned to take the ones of the poacher back to the Director before they left the city.

Suddenly two strange men came running toward them. One man grabbed the envelope of photographs from Kira's hand. Then they ran into the crowded street.

"Come back, thief!" Kira cried. She and Barbie chased the men but soon lost them. There were just too many people and too many places to hide along the busy market street.

"I can't believe it!" said Kira. The girls walked back to the Land Rover. They were mad.

"Are you thinking what I'm thinking?" asked Barbie.

"What's that?" asked Kira.

"I don't think those were everyday robbers," said Barbie. "I think they were the poachers, and they stole those pictures on purpose."

"How did they know where we were?" said Kira.

"They must have been following us," said Barbie. "The man you photographed yesterday must have known it. He told the others and they waited for us. They probably followed us from the reserve."

"We're going to have to be a lot more careful," said Kira. "I'm so mad that they got all those pictures."

"Oh, no!" cried Barbie.

"What is it?" asked Kira.

"Look," Barbie said. All four tires on the Land Rover were flat.

"It's going to take us hours to get new tires and get back to the reserve," said Kira. "These poachers are really awful."

"Yes," said Barbie. "And I don't think they'll stop bothering us until they get the baby elephant."

"Do you think they'll try to steal him while only Ken and Jim are there?" said Kira.

"I think that's exactly what they'll try to do," said Barbie.

"But we'll never get back there in time to warn them," said Kira.

"Wait," said Barbie. "I think I have a plan."

"What?" Kira asked.

"First let's go back to the Director," said Barbie. "We should tell him all about this. Then we can use his radio to get in touch with Ken and Jim. I hope."

"What if we can't reach them?" asked Kira.

"I'll think of something," said Barbie. "There is no way those poachers are going to get our baby elephant. No way at all."

7

A Nasty Surprise

The girls ran all the way to the Director's office.

"The poachers cut our tires," Barbie explained. The Director was as angry as Kira and Barbie.

"They won't get away with any more of this," said the Director. "We will catch those troublemakers!" He called the rangers' station and told them what was happening.

"They will send a jeep out to your camp right away," he said.

"We'd like to use your radio to reach Jim and Ken," Barbie said.

"Go ahead," said the Director. Barbie tried calling on the radio, but there was no answer.

"They must have left camp," said Barbie.

"Maybe they went for a hike, or to get more

water," said Kira.

"Or maybe they were chased away," said Barbie. "We've got to get back there—fast."

"You can take my van," said the Director. "My driver can get you there as quickly as anyone and then bring my car back. By then yours will have been repaired and I will send another ranger out with it."

"Thank you so much," said Barbie. The Director made a few phone calls and everything was set. Soon Barbie and Kira were sitting in the van, speeding back to the game reserve.

"I hope we get there in time," said Barbie.

"In time for what?" wondered Kira.

"I'm not sure," answered Barbie. She was worried that the poachers might steal the elephant or hurt Ken or Jim. Even though the driver went as fast as he could, it seemed like this trip to the reserve took forever.

Finally they arrived at the camp. It was

empty. It was also a mess. The poachers had obviously been there and not found the elephant.

"They must have been so angry they just wrecked everything," said Barbie. The tents had been pulled down. Food from the cooler was thrown out on the ground. Water jugs had been cut open.

"But where are Ken and Jim and the elephant?" asked Kira.

"I wonder if they even know about this," said Barbie. "Maybe they were already gone when the poachers came here."

"Then the poachers could be after them," said Kira. "They could still be in danger."

"We've got to find them first," said Barbie. "But how—"

"I am a good tracker," said the van driver. "I can help you find your friends."

"That's a great idea," said Barbie. "But I think we'll need more help than that. Can we call the rangers on the van's radio?"

"Yes," said the driver.

"Let's see if we can get a helicopter to help find Ken and Jim," said Barbie. "First we'll need to have some idea of where they went." The driver, Martin, got out of the van and checked around the camp. When he was sure which way the guys had gone with the elephant, he told Barbie. She called the rangers and asked for help.

"They said they would try to get a helicopter out as soon as possible," said Barbie. "Should we try to follow the tracks?"

"I think they were probably heading for the river. That's elephant country," said Martin. "We can drive there in the van to save time."

"What if that's not where they went?" said Kira.

"We will know that soon enough," said Martin. "Then we will try the second place they might have gone."

"How can you tell where they went from a few tracks?" asked Barbie.

"It's not the tracks," said Martin. "I know Jim. I know the places he would go if he were trying to find elephants. There are a few places close enough to check."

"Let's go then," said Barbie. She looked back at their ruined campsite as the van drove away. "I'm not sure we'll be able to camp here tonight," she said.

"I'm not sure I want to," said Kira.

"Unless those poachers are caught today," said Martin, "it won't be safe for you to camp there anyway."

"Well, I hope they are caught," said Barbie. "And not because of what they did to our camp. Not even because they stole our pictures. I hope they get caught before they hurt any more animals."

"Especially one small elephant," said Kira.

"And two friends," said Barbie. The van

moved quickly over the bumpy road, but it didn't seem quick enough. The girls were really worried. It was a great relief when the river finally came into sight.

"Look!" Barbie cried. "I think I see them." On the far side of the river they could see two people walking. But where was the baby elephant?

8

To the Rescue

"Ken! Jim!" Barbie called. The van had crossed the river but couldn't follow the guys into the bush where they were headed. Barbie jumped out as soon as the van stopped and ran after them.

"How did you find us?" asked Ken.

"We had a little help," said Barbie.

"What's wrong?" Ken asked. Kira and Martin joined the group.

"Well, now that we know you're okay, probably nothing," said Barbie. "Except that a bunch of really angry poachers are after you."

"Tell us everything," said Jim. Barbie and Kira explained about the stolen pictures and the cut tires on their Land Rover. Then they described the mess back at their camp. "It is worse than I expected," said Jim. "I think we should leave the reserve."

"And just give up?" said Barbie. "Wait a second." Barbie looked all around. "Where is he?" she asked. "The elephant…"

"Oh, don't worry," said Ken. "We left him in a safe place."

"We wanted to be sure there wasn't anyone poaching near the river before we brought him out for a bath and a drink," said Jim.

"But that's terrible!" said Barbie. "If they were following you, they could have found the elephant already."

"Come on," said Ken. He started running down the path.

"Martin and I can stay here with the van," said Kira. "I'd like to get some pictures of the river anyway."

"Good idea," said Barbie. "We'll meet up back here as soon as we know something. Bye." Barbie ran after Ken and Jim who were already on their way. When they got to the little clearing they saw lots of broken trees and large footprints in the mud, but no elephant.

"Oh, no," said Barbie. "They've taken him away. We're too late!"

"Maybe not," said Jim. "We can try to follow them. It isn't easy to hide the tracks of an elephant." He found a path through the brush and pointed. "They went this way."

"Do you think they've gone far?" Barbie asked.

"No," said Ken. "We were gone for only ten minutes."

"Unless they had a van," said Jim. "If they followed us on foot, they haven't gone far. But if they took the elephant in that van—"

"Then we're out of luck," said Barbie. "I'm going back to the river. There's a helicopter out looking for you. Maybe it can find the baby elephant or the poachers' van." She ran back to Kira and Martin as fast as she could. She was out of breath by the time she got to the van.

"What happened?" asked Kira.

"Nothing," panted Barbie. "But we need to radio the rangers in the helicopter." She rested for another minute then got on the radio. When she had told them about the poachers, she called to Martin and Kira. "We can drive to meet Ken and Jim. If they find the elephant, they'll need our help to deal with the poachers. If not—"

"Then what?" Kira asked.

"I'm not sure," said Barbie. "Let's hope we don't have to find out." They all got in the van and Martin took off at top speed.

"What's that?" Barbie cried out. Ahead of them was a thick cloud of dust. It was impossible to see what was causing it.

"It's not moving fast enough to be the van," said Martin. "I think the poachers may be running with the elephant."

"Let's get them," said Barbie.

"But what about Ken and Jim?" Kira said.

Just then the two ran out of the bush.

"There they are!" Barbie said. "Hurry!" Martin sped up. Soon he passed Ken and Jim. As he got closer to the dust cloud, everyone could see it was caused by four men running. They were shouting and clapping their hands to make the baby elephant run too. Martin drove ahead of the poachers and cut them off.

"We've got them!" Kira and Barbie cried. Quickly they all got out of the van. Ken and Jim rushed up from behind.

"Go away," yelled the tallest poacher. It was the same man who had tried to steal the elephant the night before. "We warned you not to stick your nose into our business."

"You will be very sorry," yelled another poacher. He was one of the thieves who had stolen Kira's photographs. The poachers looked dangerous. They wanted to fight. Then suddenly a loud sound filled the air. Everyone looked up. It was the rangers' helicopter.

"Run!" yelled the tallest poacher. The other poachers followed him into the thickest part of the bush. Ken, Jim and Martin tried to follow, but the poachers had disappeared without a trace.

9

Trapped!

"Is he all right?" Barbie asked. A vet from the rangers' station had come in the helicopter to see the elephant.

"He's very tired. He needs rest and water," said the vet. "But the cut on his back is not deep."

"Does that mean he'll be okay?" asked Kira.

"Yes," said the vet. "If he gets some care." He scratched the little elephant behind the ears.

"We'd like to take care of him," said Barbie. "But we've got a problem."

"A few problems," said Kira. "Like no camp. And a bunch of angry, mean poachers who are going to be even angrier and meaner."

"We have no choice but to leave the reserve tonight," said Jim.

"But we can't leave him," Barbie said. "I

think we should stay."

"But those poachers are going to come after us," said Ken.

"Yes," said Barbie. "And when they do, we'll be ready for them." Barbie explained her plan to the group. When she had finished, Martin left in the helicopter with the vet and the rangers.

"Good luck," he called. He waved good-bye to his new friends.

Soon Barbie and the others were driving back to the camp in Martin's van.

"Oh dear," said Jim. "This is going to take some time to fix up." Barbie had used the radio in the van to call the ranger station to ask for help. The rangers had agreed to send some new water jugs, food and other supplies.

"I guess we should start by getting the tents back up," said Barbie. "I'm going to call the Director back in the city and tell him that Martin is returning." Barbie radioed the

Director of Wildlife Services and told him what had happened. She also told him their plan.

"I think it might work," said the Director. "But be very careful. I'll make sure you get everything you need." Barbie finished talking and quickly joined in to help clean up the camp.

"All right," said Barbie. "At least we've got someplace to sleep tonight." The tents were up, but the cots were broken. The rest of their things were thrown all over.

"Remember how calm things seemed last night?" said Kira.

"They won't be quiet tonight," Barbie said with a smile. "But I guess we can have a nice dinner and sit around the campfire for a while." Soon everyone was helping to make a vegetable stew. While it was cooking, they gathered more wood for a fire.

"Oh, look," Kira cried. "Someone is coming." It was the large truck from the rangers' station. It pulled to a stop in front of the camp.

"We're so glad to see you!" said Barbie. Soon the whole group was unloading the truck. There were a fresh supply of food and new cots. There were also four very large water barrels. Two of them were so heavy that Ken and Jim had to carry them together. There were also two big crates full of pots and pans.

"I'll just take these around behind the tents," said Barbie.

She carried one crate. Kira carried the other. The baby elephant was tied by a long rope to a tree. He was happily munching leaves.

"Well, the barrels are all in place," said Ken. "I guess we're ready." They all went back to say good-bye to the rangers.

"We'll be keeping a close watch where the poachers won't see us," said one ranger.

"Thanks," said Barbie. The truck drove away.

"Time to eat," called Jim. It was getting dark

when they sat down at the table.

"Do you think they're watching us?" Kira whispered to Barbie.

"I don't know," Barbie answered. Sooner or later the poachers would find out that they had returned to camp.

When they had all finished eating, they moved to sit around the campfire. They talked about their exciting day.

"I'll go take care of the last few details," Ken said. He left the group and disappeared behind the tents. There were some rattling noises and Ken returned. "Well, that's done."

"There's nothing left to do now but wait," said Kira. Barbie and Jim practiced the beautiful African song he had taught her the night before.

"This is the best thing that has happened all day," said Barbie. She looked up at the bright stars and yawned. "Oh, excuse me," she said. "I'm so sleepy."

"It has been a long day," said Ken. Everyone was ready to get to bed. They put out the fire and headed for the tents.

"Keep your fingers crossed," whispered Barbie. "We should know soon if our plan is going to work." Barbie lay in bed listening. She was tired, but she tried to stay awake. It was so hard to keep her eyes open. She was just about to fall asleep when there was a loud crash and the sound of someone yelling.

10

Home At Last

"Let's go!" Barbie cried. She jumped out of bed. She was still wearing her shorts and shirt. Kira was still dressed too. The girls grabbed their flashlights and ran out of the tent. They were joined by Martin, Ken and Jim. Behind the tents they heard shouting.

"We've caught one of them," said a ranger. He and another ranger had been hiding in the water barrels. Ken had scattered the two crates full of pots and pans all over the ground. When the poacher tried to get to the baby elephant, the rangers heard him trip on the pans. Then they jumped out of the barrels and caught him.

"Now let's see if those rangers can get the others," said Jim. A few minutes later, the rangers arrived in their truck. They had two other poachers in handcuffs.

"It looks as if a couple got away, but we'll have them soon enough," said a ranger. He climbed into the truck. It sped away into the night.

"I'm glad to see the last of them," said Barbie.

"Me too," said Kira.

"How about some tea around the fire?" Jim asked. No one could go back to bed after so much excitement. They settled around the fire to talk and sip tea.

"But what about the others in the gang?" Kira asked.

"The three they caught will probably give away where the others are hiding," said Jim.

"And even if they don't," said Ken, "I don't think they would bother us after tonight." Everyone laughed. It had been a little scary, but now that the elephant was safe and the poachers were going to jail, they felt better.

"Tomorrow we can actually go on that photo safari," said Barbie. Soon the fire was put out and everyone went back to the tents. This time Barbie fell asleep as soon as her head hit the pillow.

They spent the next day driving and hiking through the reserve, taking hundreds of pictures. Jim was right. Once he took them to the right spots, there were lots of animals to see. Hippos, rhinos, giraffes, gazelles, lions, hyenas, zebras and more. They returned to camp and soon got a message over the radio that made them even happier.

"The Director has found a place for our baby elephant," cried Barbie. "Tomorrow we're to take him to his new home."

"And what about those awful poachers?" asked Kira.

"He said they have all been put in jail," said Barbie. "At least they won't be hurting any more animals."

Early the next morning, Ken, Kira, Jim and Barbie packed up their camp and left the game reserve. The Director had sent Martin back with a large truck to carry the elephant.

"Oh, Barbie," Martin said. "Here is a letter that came for you." While Ken and Martin got the baby elephant into the truck, Barbie opened the letter.

"It's from Midge," said Barbie.

"What's so important that she couldn't wait until you got home?" asked Kira.

"This is great," said Barbie. "Midge got the ice cream shop she's wanted forever! The grand opening is planned for three weeks from now."

"How is she going to get everything ready so fast?" asked Ken.

"Well," said Barbie with a laugh, "she's expecting a little help." Ken laughed too.

"Did she write to be sure you wouldn't stay an extra week or two in Africa?" asked Kira.

"No," said Barbie. "But she really does need our help. And most important, she wants us to be part of her dream-come-true. That's what having the ice cream shop means to her."

"That's really nice," said Kira.

"But right now," said Barbie, "we've got a little elephant to worry about." She put the letter away. Martin was waiting in the truck. Jim, Kira, Barbie and Ken climbed into the Land Rover and they were on their way. The elephant stuck his trunk out the back of the truck and waved at his friends driving in the Land Rover behind him.

"Silly elephant," said Barbie. "I wonder what he thinks of all this."

"He will be very happy on Mrs. Radding's farm," said Jim. Mrs. Radding was an older woman who had a huge farm. She used a large part of her land to take care of injured wild animals. When they were recovered they went back to the game reserve.

"My wish finally came true," said Barbie. She and her friends watched happily as the baby elephant stepped out of the truck to his new home. Mrs. Radding was a kind lady. She greeted the elephant with a pat on the head and a juicy apple.

"What wish?" asked Ken.

"Remember that first night we watched the sunset?" Barbie said.

"And you wished on the wishing star..." said Ken.

"I wished we could find a good home for our baby elephant," said Barbie. Before they left Barbie gave the elephant a hug. "Thanks for making it such an exciting trip," she said.

"Barbie, you're the best," said Ken.